ATTACK OF THE VAMPIRATES

Ace just pointed. The other bats followed his finger. They had reached the end of the tunnel and were looking down into an enormous cavern, lit by pale moonlight. A sea-water lake shimmered between patches of mist below, reflecting ripples of light that washed over the cave walls. A sudden breeze cleared the mist from the lake surface and the bats gasped when they saw where Ace's finger was aiming. There, rising up from the water like a scaly sea-monster, was a dark, three-masted ship…

Look out for:
Revenge of the Vampirates

Hippo Adventure

ATTACK OF THE VAMPIRATES

Martin Oliver

Hippo

Scholastic Children's Books,
7–9 Pratt Street, London NW1 0AE, UK
a division of Scholastic Publications Ltd
London ~ New York ~ Toronto ~ Sydney ~ Auckland

First published by Scholastic Publications Ltd, 1993
This edition published by Scholastic Publications Ltd, 1995

ISBN 0 590 55934 6

Typeset by TW Typesetting, Midsomer Norton, Avon

Printed by Cox & Wyman Ltd, Reading, Berks

10 9 8 7 6 5 4 3 2 1

For Andrea

Chapter 1

Small fish darted out of the way of the tall, dark ship as it slipped silently through the calm sea. Silhouetted by the grey moonlight, three masts stuck up like bony fingers from the black hull. The ship was surrounded by an eerie silence and an air of brooding menace. No seagulls ever followed this boat into harbour, no dolphins ever dived and frolicked in its wake. A flag with a sinister design hung limply above the mainmast, and strangest of all, the ship cast no shadow on the sea.

High up in the crow's nest a look-out hissed "land ahoy"! A black shape, gold glittering from each shoulder, detached itself from the decks below and stared through a telescope at the group of islands ahead. The captain of the strange vessel quickly checked over five small rocky outcrops then focused on the largest island. The telescope slowly moved from the west shore, stopping to rest for a second on the large mountain rising from the centre of the island before moving east towards the inland trees and bushes that were groaning under the weight of all sorts of luscious fruits.

"This is the place," the captain chuckled to his shadowy crew. "I know where we can drop anchor. There's a cave inside the cliff dead ahead. No one will find us there."

The ship sailed towards the wall of sheer rock and was swallowed up in the blackness. Seconds later the anchor splashed into the water and a distant echo escaped out of the mouth of the cave and floated over the sea towards the nearest island…

"Fruit Isle Welcomes Carefulll Flyers," squeaked a high-pitched voice. It belonged to a small fruitbat who was hanging from a ledge, proudly reading the banner he had just painted in dripping, uneven letters. He dropped his brush into the pot, watching it gradually sink into the thick paint.

"Not bad, though I say it myself," he muttered, standing back to admire his handiwork.

"Oh, yes, very nice, Radar," one of his neighbours replied, poking her head out of one of the many caves that honeycombed the slopes of the mountain which was home to the fruitbats. "Sorry I can't stay and chat – I'm in a bit of a flap. We've got so much to do, I've never known so much work for the fruit festival."

Radar sighed in agreement. This year there was a bumper crop of fruit on the island and every single fruitbat had been buzzing for weeks. The sky near the mountain was black with bats flying hither and thither. They were collecting and carrying fruit in preparation for the annual fruit festival which would take place in two nights' time.

As well as fly-pasts and gravity-defying aerobatic displays over the mountains of fresh fruit, there was something extra special about the festival. It was the highlight of the bats' year, a glittering social occasion – literally.

Radar shivered with nervous excitement as he tried to picture the solemn ceremony that took place just before the festival was due to commence. Through a maze of winding, dark tunnels – a secret route handed down for generations – the ten eldest bats on Fruit Isle, known as the Flight Leaders, flew to a cave hidden deep inside the mountain. In the darkest corner of the cave was a heavy chest, thick with dust, wrapped in chains and locked with ten sturdy padlocks. It was rumoured that, a hundred years ago, the sea–chest had been washed up on the island along with a bunch of rusty keys. Radar knew that each of the Flight Leaders carried one of these keys with them at all times. In his mind's eye, Radar saw the keys being inserted into the locks and then, at exactly the same time, turned 90 degrees. Only then did the heavy lid of the chest spring open, revealing the treasures that lay within.

Radar remembered the thrill that danced across his wings every time the Flight Leaders reappeared, laden down with the precious objects: rubies, red like apples; pearls and emeralds as big as grapes; gold and diamonds all glistening under the moon.

Each of the bats poured their share of the treasure into ten large bowls that were dotted around the beach where the festival took place. Greens, reds and yellows danced in a cascade of colour until the bowls were full. Then Albat, the most senior of the leaders, would get shakily to his feet and say:

"We have shown you one sort of our island's treasure, now it is time to enjoy another kind. Let the fruit festival begin."

Radar licked his lips in anticipation and was reaching out to take a handful of food, when…

"There's only one 'l' in careful, you idiot." A shrill voice shattered Radar's dream and caused a small landslide of rocks high up on the mountain. Radar snapped back to reality as he looked around and came face to face with Aunt Bathilda. She looked at him over her half-moon glasses. "Still, at least you've tried to do some work, unlike that bunch of lazy layabats you hang around with."

"Yikes," gasped Radar. Aunt Bathilda had reminded him there was a Fruit Gang meeting at midnight. He had been so busy dreaming that it had slipped his mind. "I'm off," he shouted, hurriedly running down the slope and taking off unsteadily. "I hope I'm not too late."

Chapter 2

"So where's Radar?" Ace asked impatiently, drumming his fingers against a branch in the tree where the gang were meeting. "We've been waiting for ages. Trust him to be late – he's probably lost."

"As usual," added a muffled voice. Ace looked across to the spot where, a few minutes ago, a large bunch of peaches had been swinging. A large fruitbat stared back at him round some shredded stalks. "Mmmmm, delicious! If Radar's not here soon, I'm going to get some ZZZZZ's in. All this eating is tiring work."

"We'll give him a few minutes more and then we'll just have to start without him," Ace decided. "In the meantime, Rocket, I expect all gang members to stay alert."

"Hold on to your hats," a third fruitbat chipped in. "I have a hunch that Radar will be here soon." Swoop swivelled round to check the night sky. He spotted a dark dot high above and recognized Radar instantly. Swoop nudged Rocket, who took a deep breath and unleashed an earsplitting whistle.

Up in the night sky Radar's heart was pounding nervously. His unique style of flying was almost a legend on Fruit Isle. Instead of strapping on "L" plates, someone had made "D" for danger cards and given them to him. At the Bat Academy he used to watch his cave-mates with envy as they wheeled and dived gracefully, especially Swoop, who was the island sky surf and aerobatic champion. Eventually Radar had asked Swoop for some extra lessons. With his help and a few sticking plasters later, he passed his flying test, but he still wasn't used to going solo.

"Concentrate now," Radar muttered to himself. "Remember what Swoop taught you: keep flat and steady. No sudden movements."

Just then his thoughts were interrupted by a piercing whistle. He looked down and spotted Rocket in the branches of a peach tree. Rocket was the largest bat in the gang, with a voice and appetite to match. He actually wasn't a very fast flyer – he had got his nickname from the speed with which he demolished food and his ability to spit out pips and stalks with jet-propelled power. Beside him, peering out from the brim of his baseball cap, was Swoop. Last of all was Ace. He was the leader of the group and the second best flyer. A gust of wind tugged at the silk scarf he always wore.

"Hello," Radar shouted. "Look at me, I'm getting the hang of this flying business." He noticed that his friends were getting closer, much closer, and they were beginning to look worried. With a gulp Radar realized he was falling. It was too late to pull out of it – he was in a nose-dive. "H … H … HELP!" he wailed as the peach tree rushed up to meet him. Radar crossed his wings for luck and closed his eyes.

On the branch below Swoop yelled out a warning to the others. "Ten o'clock, bat coming out of the moon – it's Radar. Look out!"

CRUNCH, CRASH, SKID, THUD. Bright lights and multi-coloured stars flew round Radar's head.

"Where am I?" he groaned, looking around. He had crash-landed into the tree where the gang had been meeting. Radar could trace his landing path by the trail of snapped twigs and crushed leaves he had left in his wake. He heard an ominous rustle above and dodged to avoid a windfall peach. He gently propped himself up against a branch for support, but instead of feeling better his head started to spin and his heart began pounding loudly. The stars in the sky above were blinking brightly while, glancing down, Radar could see the ground through the leaves. Something was very wrong.

A swift 180-degree turn and Radar began to feel much better. Dangling happily beneath the branch he peered around. Down below, two piles of leaves suddenly moved then flew up towards him.

"Congratulations on another Radar roller-coaster landing," Ace smiled sourly. "We're so glad you could make it to the meeting, but next time could you do it a bit slower? We might have a chance to get out of the way then!"

Radar went red. "I … I'm sorry. I didn't mean…"

Swoop winked at him. "Don't worry, you'll soon get used to that left turn – just keep the right wing steady."

Swoop turned to Ace. "There's no harm done, and at least he managed to wake up Rocket."

The fruitbats stared at each other. Where was Rocket? He had vanished.

"Ssh, listen." Ace's ears pricked up. He could hear a muffled sound. Where was it coming from? "After me."

Ace dived down to a splattered peach, closely followed by Swoop. Radar landed with a thud beside them.

"We've got to get him out from under there," Ace yelled urgently. "He could be hurt."

Radar frantically pulled at the fruit, but his fingers kept slipping off the soggy mulch. Ace took charge and began positioning the others. They each took a piece of the peach skin. "Now!" he ordered. The three fruitbats took the strain. Beating their wings furiously they strained to shift the squashed fruit. At last it began to move, but what would they find underneath? What state would Rocket be in?

"Oh, no, not you lot," Rocket groaned loudly. "Why did you have to go and rescue me? I'm fine, I was eating my way to safety."

"What a bunch," Ace sighed, rolling his eyes skywards. "Can we start the meeting now?"

"What about Rocket?" Swoop asked. "He might be in shock."

To answer the question, Rocket stuck out his tongue and with a loud slurp, licked himself clean.

"Despite the fact that our old hide-out is no longer operational," Ace began, looking pointedly at Radar, "I declare the meeting open. Let's get straight down to business. At the moment, all we have is a name – The Fruit Gang – but to be a proper gang we need to think up lots of other things. We should have a motto and secret passwords for bat ears only. We could make disguises or have a secret sign that only we know."

"Oh, I get it," Swoop said. "What about a warning whistle? One long blast followed by two shorter ones. If we hear the whistle it means one of us is in trouble and the others must drop whatever they're doing and fly to the rescue. Agreed?"

Radar kept quiet as Rocket nodded eagerly. He'd better not tell the others that he couldn't whistle.

"Excellent idea," Ace said. "Anyone else?"

"I've thought up a password. What about 'look out, Radar's landing'?"

"Oh, very funny, Rocket," Radar replied. He could see the others were looking at him expectantly. It must be his turn. Help! Radar panicked. He blurted out the first thing that came into his head. "How about this for our motto – 'Is it a bird? Is it a plane? No, it's the Fruit Gang...' No? ... Just give me a bit more time ... er ... what do you think of 'Batabunga' as our war-cry?"

"Where on earth did they come from?" Ace

sighed. "I think they need some work. OK, next."

"I've come up with two ideas for a war-cry – 'Bat Attack', or 'Bat Blast'."

"Thank you, Swoop. Not bad at all. Now what about passwords? We could use names of fruits and change them each meeting."

"Sounds good to me. I've thought of a motto. How about this? 'They fly by night and arrive with a bang. Don't mess with these guys, they're the fruitbat gang'."

Radar kept quiet as the meeting carried on. He was sure he had some good ideas but he didn't dare speak out in case no one liked them. He listened to the others' suggestions until eventually Ace glanced at the slowly fading moon.

"We must stop as it's nearly dawn. Tomorrow we'll rendezvous here at the same time. Your mission is to think up something useful for the gang. Bring along disguises or anything else you dream up. The password for tomorrow's meeting is 'pineapples' and our war-cry is 'Bat Attack'. These are our first official secrets. If anyone blabs them to non-Fruit Gang members…"

"Their punishment is to have Radar's aunt 'talkture' them for an hour! That would be about the worst thing to do to anyone." The bats agreed with Swoop and, still chuckling, flew back to their caves.

Chapter 3

The sun was just beginning to peep over the horizon when Radar landed safely on a narrow ledge halfway up the mountain. The rock face glowed with dawn redness and he was glad to squeeze into his cool, dark cave home. He brushed past a fruitbat who opened one eye and stared at him.

"Where've you been then? Playing with your little gang?"

"Shut up, elephant ears!" Radar replied crossly. His big brother was always poking his nose into other people's business. He was just jealous. Settling into a comfortable position on the cave roof, Radar yawned hugely then fell asleep with visions of giant pineapples swirling through his brain …

The next evening Radar was down early and, armed with a pot of white paint, set about correcting his banner. He enjoyed painting, liked dipping the brush into the pot and watching the white tide rise up the bristles. He whistled happily as he dolloped some paint over the offending "l"s then watched them disappear under smooth brush strokes. While he was blending in the colour to match the background, thoughts bubbled in his mind. *Fruit Gang disguises sound like fun, but what could we use?*

Suddenly, Radar had a brainwave. Of course! It was simple. Why hadn't he thought of it before? They would be ideal, but where had he put them? Radar flew across the cave and dived down into a large trunk marked "usefulll things". It was nearly midnight when he found what he was searching for. Carefully packing his finds in a bag, he set off…

Radar joined Swoop and Rocket beside their ex-HQ. They waited as Ace disappeared up into the tree he had selected as their new hide-out. Then he shouted down.

"Each of you fly up in turn and don't forget to whisper… What's the password?"

"Pineapples."

"OK, Swoop, you're in. Next one… What's the password?"

"This is silly! You know it's me… OK, OK, the password is lovely ripe, delicious, yummy … pineapples."

"About time too. Last one… What's the password?"

"Oh no, my mind's gone blank. Um, er, crab-apples. Wait a minute – it's on the tip of my tongue. Apples? No, it's apricots…"

"That's three guesses you've had and you're

not getting any more. Rules are rules. You can't come in."

"What rules?"

"The rules I've just made up. Go on now, hop it."

"But … but look, it's me, Radar."

"That's what you say, but you don't know the password. You could be an imposter. What if you're a spy disguised as Radar who wants to infiltrate our gang and steal our secrets? We can't take the risk of letting you in. You'd better disappear while we have the meeting."

Radar's wings drooped around him. It wasn't fair, he was always being picked on because he was small and wasn't very good at flying. He listened hard and heard mutterings from the branches nearby – they HAD started without him. He was about to glide home sadly when he thought about the nasty comments he would get from his brother. What a night he was going to have. "Come on, Ace. Let me in, please," he pleaded.

Ace's head appeared. "Oh, so you're still here. What do you want? I hope you're not eavesdropping, Mr Spy. You'd better be careful in case we decide to torture you to discover who you're working for."

At that moment, Rocket's head popped up with an interested expression on his face. "In fact, I think that is a good idea," Ace continued. "Get him, Rocket. We could do with some water torture practice."

"No, no, don't do that," Radar answered. "I can prove I'm me. I know things that no one else could know. For instance, when Swoop was giving me flying lessons, I crashed thirty-three times. Look, here's the scar left when I landed against a cliff, instead of on it."

"He's got a point." Swoop winced at the memory. "Radar and I are the only people who could know that."

But Ace wasn't convinced yet, he wanted more. Radar racked his brains. "I know that Rocket can't stand the sight of plums because he was so ill after eating three trees full of them –" Swoop and Ace burst out laughing – "and that Ace's middle names are Algernon Dolittle Peabody."

There was stunned silence for a second. Ace went red. "That's not true … how did you know? … I'll kill my sister," he blustered while Swoop and Rocket whooped with laughter. "Shut up, you two," Ace yelled crossly. "OK, OK, you've proved who you are, but you still can't get in without the password."

Radar concentrated. This was his second chance, he mustn't blow it. He stared around for inspiration. Out of the corner of his eye he spotted Swoop soundlessly moving his lips. What was he saying?

"Just give me a second," Radar said to gain extra time. He watched Swoop's mouth. Pinecones, no. Limeapples, what were they? Suddenly it clicked. "I know," Radar shouted. "The password is PINEAPPLES."

"You're supposed to whisper," Ace muttered

crossly. "Still at least you got there eventually. I suppose you can join in for now, just make sure you know the password next time." Radar covered half of his face in a mock salute to Ace while he smiled gratefully at Swoop at the same time.

Ace ignored Radar's gesture as he continued. "We'll pick up where we were before the interruption. I was about to ask for progress reports on yesterday's missions. Who's first? Any volunteers?"

Swoop began by producing a badge. He had drawn a picture of a black bat flying past the moon and stuck it on to the front.

"This is my idea for a secret badge," he said. "But that's not all," he continued. "I thought a secret badge deserves a secret pocket. And here's one that I made earlier." Swoop unzipped his jacket and showed the others a pocket he had sewn under his wing. "No one would ever think of looking there. We could all have a secret pocket to carry our gang gear in. What do you think?"

"It would certainly be handy for emergency food rations," said Rocket eagerly. "Though I might need some more secret pockets… Now, here's something I thought up." He flashed four scraps of paper with scrawled stick-bat pictures at the gang. "Identity cards," he explained proudly. "All the best gangs have them. I also think we need some dead letter drops – secret places like hollow trees where we can leave messages for other gang members."

"Good work, you two," smiled Ace. "You've obviously been thinking hard. Now it's Radar's turn."

Radar's heart beat quickly as he began the speech he had been practising in his head. "I woke up this evening thinking about disguises and I first asked myself what makes a good disguise?"

"Something that hides your ugly mug?" volunteered Rocket. "Owww!" He rubbed his ribs where Swoop elbowed him.

"A good disguise should be easy to carry and quick to put on." Radar paused to glance at the others. He was pleased to see that now they were all concentrating. "That ruled out all my initial ideas like big overcoats and hats. It seemed impossible…" Radar heard a sigh of disappointment escape from Ace. "But then I had a brainwave. I came up with a disguise that fits into your pocket, that passes the quick change test and ties in with our secret identities as members of the Fruit Gang. One minute I'm Radar, the next…" He swivelled round, put something on his face then turned back to face the others. "I'm in disguise. TA DA!"

Ace winced, Swoop's jaw dropped and Rocket nearly keeled over. "What do you think then?" There was silence for a few seconds as the Fruit Gang stared at Radar's disguise. He had almost disappeared behind an enormous pair of sunglasses. The lenses were a normal black colour, but the frames were bright banana yellow and the corners were shaped like lemons.

"I've got one orange, one strawberry and one pineapple pair. They fit in with our passwords and everything. They were a Christmas present from Aunt Bathilda. I wondered what they might be useful for..." Radar's voice trailed off as he took off the glasses and saw the expressions on the others' faces.

Swoop recovered first. "They ... they're very, er, very ... interesting. The theory behind them is great. It's just that they're ... um..."

"They're hideous!" Rocket waded in. "I wouldn't be seen dead in them."

"They're not exactly inconspicuous. If we wore those, we certainly wouldn't fade into the background. Everyone would be staring at us, and that's not the idea of a good disguise. All that trouble to get into the meeting and that's the only thing you come up with... It's useless."

Radar bit his lip and shoved the glasses back into the bag. Swoop tried to rescue Radar by changing the subject. "Come on, let's forget all this stuff for a bit. A proper gang should stop talking and start having some adventures. So, what can we do? Something exciting."

Radar's brain raced. I'll show them, he thought. I'll prove that I'm the best bat here!

"Let's go to Black Island," he said loudly. Rocket turned pale and Ace gulped. Black Island was a windswept place a few minutes' flying away. It was made of jagged, black volcanic rock. Nothing grew on the island except for sharp thistles and thorn bushes. Waves constantly battered the shores, making caves and passages in the cliffs through which the wind howled. Fruitbats avoided the place and strange whispered stories told of ghosts and spooky shadows.

"A fine gang you are," Radar said. "Stay

here if you're too scared – I'm out of here."
And without waiting to see if the others were
following, Radar took off.

Chapter 4

Hovering over Black Island, Radar felt his courage draining away. The island looked even more barren and uninviting than he had imagined – in fact it looked rather like one of Aunt Bathilda's fruit cakes. It was a strange shape, as if it had been made by a giant hand that had gathered rocks, stones and soil, scrunched them all together and left the mixture to bake in the sun. It sloped steeply from left to right, just like Aunt Bathilda's latest creation, which had risen patchily and which Radar had hidden along with the others in the darkest part of his cave. From his viewpoint in the air, he could see that the waves had sliced off a piece of island and were biting into the cliffs. Blackened boulders scattered about the island looked just like the burnt sultanas his aunt used as "decoration". They probably tasted the same too.

Radar grinned for a second as he remembered how Bathilda's cakes had even defeated Rocket, leaving him grounded for a week. Then his face became serious as he thought about why he was there. He couldn't turn back, but at least there was no sign of any ghosts. I'll just do a quick explore and grab a rock to prove I was here, he thought to himself.

Spotting a good landing spot near the edge of a cliff, Radar began descending. His feet were just on the verge of touching down when a tail wind whipped up from nowhere and blew him off target.

Don't panic! Radar thought, panicking. He tried to straighten his wings, but the wind was so strong he was blown right off the cliff. The ground disappeared from under him and he began to fall. He flapped his wings but couldn't pull out of the dive. Rocks whistled past in a blur, waves crashed on the rocks below. Down, down, down he plummeted. He closed his eyes, bracing himself for the inevitable crash ... then suddenly he felt a strong grip on his wings and sensed himself gliding upwards. Radar opened his eyes and saw three familiar faces – Swoop, Ace and Rocket. They flew him on to a narrow ledge below a cave.

"Thanks, you guys," Radar managed to whisper between breaths.

"It's OK," Swoop said. "We owed you a favour after the glasses episode. Quits?"

Radar nodded gratefully and the others smiled. "I feel better already. I'm glad it's all sorted ... orted ... rted." His voice bounced off the cliff-face and echoed round the cave above.

"Well, if Radar's OK, what are we waiting for?" The bats followed Ace and hovered in formation outside the cave entrance. It looked like a huge mouth – smooth, curved rocks formed the lips and stalactites speared down from the roof like sharp fangs, yellowed with age. Reddy brown water spiralled down the rock teeth and drip, drip, dripped on to the floor below. Inside, the cave was arched and led downwards like a giant's throat. The bats wrinkled their noses as a strong smell of rotting seaweed and salt-water blew towards them.

"What a whiff," Swoop complained. "I bet it leads down to the sea."

"It could do with a tidal mouth-rinse," Rocket grinned. Ace flapped ahead of the others, keen to lead the way. Gliding between stalactites and soaring over slippery stones, the Fruit Gang darted through the tunnel as it sloped down and round. Soon the sound of waves breaking echoed towards them and they could almost taste salt on their lips.

"I reckon we'll reach the sea just round this corner," Ace whispered. He accelerated round the bend then, without warning, slammed on the air anchors. BANG, THUNK, CRUNCH. The trio behind piled-up into Ace. They stayed up in the air for a second before dropping to the floor where they rolled around in a muddled huddle of wings, heads and legs.

Swoop spat one of Rocket's size ten feet out of his mouth and struggled to untangle himself from the others.

"What did you do that for?" he angrily asked Ace. "Don't just stand there with that stupid expression on your face, say something."

But Ace didn't reply, he just pointed. The other bats followed his finger. They had reached the end of the tunnel and were looking down into an enormous cavern, lit by pale moonlight. A sea-water lake shimmered between patches of mist below, reflecting ripples of light that washed over the cave walls. A sudden breeze cleared the mist from the lake surface and the bats gasped when they saw where Ace's finger was aiming. There, rising up from the water like a scaly sea-monster, was a dark, three-masted ship...

Chapter 5

Radar was first to break the silence.

"It's just some old wreck," he whispered, trying to keep his voice steady. "There's nothing to explore here. Let's just leave quietly."

"Hold on a minute." Ace grabbed the rapidly retreating bat. "I think this is it – our big chance for an adventure. That's no ordinary ship."

The Fruit Gang silently studied the boat. Cobwebs hung over the black hull and its sails were ragged and patched. The stern decks reared up like a tall, forbidding tower; shuttered portholes and cannon-ports stared blindly at the bats. Radar shivered – he had the feeling he was being watched although no one was on the deck.

Swoop strained to make out some painted letters on the green-barnacled bows. "*The Black Fang* is a strange name for a boat – and look at that figurehead."

Radar gasped as he spotted a huge skeleton with grasping hands leaping out from the bows.

"What a toothy grin," he muttered. "I wouldn't like him to be smiling at me."

How had the vessel got there? Did it have a crew, and why did they have such a strange ship? Questions flashed through Ace's brain, but before he could answer them, Swoop spotted movement atop the main mast. At first it looked like an ordinary, slightly ragged flag, but then he spotted its horrible design.

"P … p … pirates!" he stuttered.

"VERY GOOD!" A loud voice boomed around the cave. "You have discovered our secret hide-out. We must get better acquainted." The fruitbats started as the tunnel behind them glowed blood-red and a shadowy shape appeared out of nowhere – it was a large bat, wearing a black cape.

"LOOK AT ME!" the bat commanded. Radar found himself staring into a pair of bloodshot eyes. He struggled to escape from the imprisoning gaze, but was caught as surely as if he had been in a bat trap. Against his will, he felt himself being pulled through the air along with Ace, Rocket and Swoop.

"My name is Blood," the bat whispered, stretching out his arms. Two brilliant white skull tattoos grinned from each wing. "I am captain of the bad ship *The Black Fang*, but there's something else. I'm also…" The bat paused and swirled his cloak around him. When Captain Blood reappeared, he seemed bigger. His face was a deathly white and his mouth parted slightly to reveal a pair of long, sharp fangs glinting with anticipation.

Radar's blood chilled in his veins. "He's a VAMPIRATE!" he wailed helplessly.

"Come closer, closer," the silent message beamed out from Blood's mesmerizing, hypnotic stare. Darkness swamped the fruit-bats' minds as they were slowly pulled towards the sinister vampirate. There was no escape.

SPLASH! A large drop of water dropped from the roof of the cave. It sprayed Ace's face then trickled coldly down his neck. Instantly he awoke from the vampirate's spell. He grabbed Rocket and pushed him against Swoop and Radar. The fruitbats bashed into each other and their eyes slipped away from Captain Blood's gaze.

"Don't look at him!" Ace yelled urgently. "Snap out of it."

As the Fruit Gang flapped unsteadily into the air, Captain Blood roared angrily.

"Vampirates arise, you scurvy swabs! Catch these intruders!" Before the echoes had died away, Swoop turned round to see dark shapes streaming out of doors and hatches on *The Black Fang*. A motley crew of vampirates, some with sharp daggers gripped between their fangs, some brandishing cutlasses, swarmed into the air.

Rocket hovered beside Ace.

"You're supposed to be our leader – what do we do now?"

Ace nodded. "I've calmly considered all the options, weighed up our alternatives, and reached the conclusion that there's only one thing to do – LET'S GET OUT OF HERE!"

The Fruit Gang needed no further encouragement and they swept past Captain Blood, searching for a way out.

"Fly like fury!" Swoop yelled. "And keep together, otherwise we'll be picked off one by one." They formed into an arrow formation, Swoop pointing the way with Radar slipstreaming behind him and Rocket and Ace acting as wing bats.

The fruitbats darted down the tunnel as the captain shouted furiously to his crew.

"Cut them off, head them off, then we'll cut off their heads." Stalactites and stalagmites whizzed past in a blur as the fruitbats flew for their lives. Radar didn't dare look behind but he could hear the flapping of wings and angry shouts getting louder – the pursuers were closing in. Up ahead, Swoop spotted moonlight.

"Nearly there, nearly there…" He broke off suddenly as sinister shapes appeared in his line of vision – vampirates were blocking their escape route.

There was only one thing to do.

"Bat attack!" Swoop yelled. "Charge!" Taken by surprise, the first line of vampirates scattered as the fruitbats cut through them. Ace ducked as a cutlass swished over his head. Rocket crashed straight into two attackers and sent them cannoning into the tunnel walls.

"Yahoo! This is fun," he yelled. "We're through."

But more vampirate reinforcements appeared ahead. Ace gulped – they were sandwiched between villains in front and behind.

"Take evasive action!" yelled Ace. "Swoop, head down that side tunnel."

Radar stared at the narrow opening to his left. It was only a metre or so away – he would never be able to turn into it in time. What could he do? In desperation, he grabbed Swoop's heels and hung on grimly. He was flung to the right as Swoop swerved sharply to his left, his wingtips scraped the side of the tunnel and then he was in the clear. Radar let go of Swoop and arrowed down the tunnel with the others. Behind them came angry shouts and loud crashes as the two groups of surprised vampirates collided with each other.

"That's won us a bit of time," Rocket gasped. "But they'll be after us soon enough. They can fly faster than us."

"You're right," Ace muttered grimly. 'We don't know what Captain Blood and his creepy crew are doing here, but I'm sure it means trouble. One of us must get away and warn the others. I'm volunteering for Operation Rearguard – to stay put and hold the vampirates as long as I can. The tunnel is narrowest here. I'd be grateful for some help, though not from Radar – he couldn't keep a hibernating hedgehog at bay."

"But—"

"There's no time to argue, they're regrouping already. Swoop, you're the best flier, so go. And please take Radar with you."

"I guess I'll stay then. What a choice!" Rocket grumbled. "You two, get going. NOW!"

As Radar took off, Swoop darted up to the roof of the tunnel and snapped off three stalactites. He dropped two down, shouting,

"Use these as swords – and good luck."

Swoop followed Radar down the tunnel then stopped to check behind. He watched Rocket and Ace beat off the first wave of vampirates, but the pirates were quick to counter and their reply was deadly accurate. SPLAT! SMACK! The fruitbats were targeted by a volley of rotten fruit, fired by pirates using their eye-patches as batapults. Then, with the fruitbats still reeling, Captain Blood led the charge. Rocket and Ace were submerged by a wave of cutlass-carrying vampirates. They swarmed over the fruitbats and sped down the tunnel.

"We're in trouble now," Swoop gasped, switching into turbo-fly. He soon caught up with Radar. Swoop shouted encouragement as he glanced nervously behind. Their pursuers were getting closer.

Would the duo get away? With every frantic flap, the fruitbats were being slowly overhauled.

Just then Swoop spotted light at the end of the tunnel. He was nearly there, but so were the vampirates. Suddenly he was overtaken. Black shapes grinned horribly as they closed in on him.

It was time for some fancy manoeuvres. Swoop parried a cutlass thrust with his stalactite sword, then corkscrewed into a large pirate's belly. He swept on, flying circles and loop-the-loops around startled villains, but Radar wasn't so lucky.

"H … help!" Swoop was only a few flaps from freedom when he heard Radar's cry. He was surrounded by a trio of large, blood-thirsty vampirates.

"I've got to rescue him," Swoop thought, turning back. One tilt of the wings and a tail adjustment later, he was next to Radar. "Get going!" he hissed. "I'll keep them busy while you fetch help."

A quick kick sent Radar flying through the air. He reached the exit and turned to see

Swoop, his stalactite sword a blur of motion. But even Swoop couldn't hold the vampirates at bay for long. He was soon surrounded and knocked to the floor.

"Now for the last one," Captain Blood roared, pointing to Radar. "He's so puny he shouldn't cause any trouble. Three of you knock him out of the sky."

"Uh oh!" Radar gulped. He turned tail and flew out into the night air. Rocks and boulders rushed by as he skimmed the island's surface. He gritted his teeth, trying to ignore his aching bones and the head wind blowing against him, but gradually he felt himself tiring. Anxiously, he looked around. Sure enough, he spotted three dots at ten o'clock. They were zeroing in for the kill.

"What can I do?" Radar thought desperately. "Better still, what would Swoop do?" Just then a dagger cut through the air and whizzed past his ears. "Help!" Radar swerved crazily to his left. A surprised vampirate hurtled past. There was a dull thud and a crater appeared where the bat had hit the ground.

"One down, two to go," Radar thought, cheered by his unexpected victory. The other vampirates watched his wobbly flying with suspicion. While they were working out if it was a decoy, Radar gained height and tried to think clearly. "Desperate times call for desperate measures. I can't outfly them, but maybe I can outmanoeuvre them."

Time was running out fast. One vampirate had overtaken Radar, then swung round and was heading straight for him. The other one was right behind and closing fast. There was only one possible escape – a Swoop Special Spin. "But I've never, ever done one successfully," Radar wailed. "I'm a gonner!"

Suddenly he felt a reassuring presence beside him and heard a familiar voice giving him instructions. Swoop must have escaped. Radar's cheer broke off as he scanned the sky

– there was no sign of his fellow fruitbat. Still he could hear the directions. Radar ignored the oncoming vampirates and pretended he was having a lesson, just like when Swoop had helped him pass his flying test. He obeyed the gentle commands. "Steady yourself, keep loose but feel every muscle. Get ready to flip your wingtips down … NOW!"

At the last second Radar did what the voice said. He felt himself hurtling down, out of reach of the vampirates' swords. "Let the left wing go limp, and bank hard with the right."

The horizon whirled round crazily as Radar spun towards a steep gorge. "Steady, steady. Straighten up." The fruitbat flew into the gorge. Down below was a rushing torrent. "Now, brake sharply with the bottom wing … glide forwards."

Radar was almost touching the rocks on either side as he whooshed sideways through the gorge. Up above, his attackers were desperately shrieking to a halt in a blur of bandannas. He had escaped!

"Yahoo!" yelled Radar ecstatically. "Not only did I get away, I also did a Swoop Special Spin followed by a sideways glide. WOW!" The sound of his triumphant shout echoed in his ears. It turned into a roar that filled the valley.

Radar looked ahead and gasped. The source of the noise was a foaming waterfall dead ahead. He was going too fast to stop. "Hel—" his desperate cry was drowned out as he flew straight into the wall of white water.

Chapter 6

Radar eventually came to, his ears still ringing with a roaring, foaming, whooshing noise. He lay still for a few moments, slowly gathering his thoughts and trying to get his bearings. Not daring to move his bruised body, his eyes darted about. He was inside a dark cave, surrounded on almost every side by sharp, damp rocks. Faint watery-grey light washed over him as it filtered into the cave through a strange white-green curtain.

Of course! Suddenly it all came flooding back. Pictures flashed through his memory.

The Black Fang moored in the cave. Captain Blood and his crew. Flying down a narrow tunnel. Swoop being captured. Doing the Swoop Special Spin. Crashing into the waterfall.

He must have blacked out, but his speed had carried him on and into the hidden cave. Radar gently checked first his head, then his wings and legs. Nothing was broken, but he was soaking wet and his teeth were chattering. Still feeling slightly dazed, he stood up cautiously and walked a few unsteady paces before losing his footing and falling to the floor. His landing was surprisingly soft. Damp, green moss covered the floor of the cave. It must have saved him from injury when he had crash-landed.

"I'm the only one left," he gulped. "The only one to get clean away."

But had he actually got away? Radar tried to peer out of the cave but he couldn't see through the waterfall. There was no way of telling if any vampirates were on guard outside, waiting for him to reappear. He pondered his next move. Although the cave was safe, he couldn't stay there for ever. Perhaps there was another way out through the tunnels that dotted Black Island. If he found it, he would quickly reach Fruit Isle.

Radar imagined himself delivering a breathless warning. Although he didn't know exactly what Blood was planning, the fruit-bats could retreat deep into the mountain and wait for the vampirates to leave. The fruitbats would be forever grateful – Aunt Bathilda would call him the hero of Fruit Isle. He might even become a Flight Leader! Radar pictured the scene as he was hoisted shoulder-high and paraded around the mountain. For once he would hog the limelight and get the credit.

But what about the Fruit Gang? Radar stopped in his tracks. His plan meant leaving Ace, Rocket and Swoop in the clutches of

Captain Blood and his crew. At this very moment they might be being tortured. Mind you, a bit of water torture would serve Ace and Rocket right after what they had threatened to do to him. They had never really treated him properly. Why should he risk his neck for them? But that left Swoop. *He* had always helped Radar. What should he do? Rescue the Fruit Gang or warn the fruitbats? As Radar searched for a way out of the cave, he wondered where Ace, Rocket and Swoop were now…

"Ouch!" Ace groaned. He was aching all over and bright lights glittered like stars in the blackness around his head. The stars suddenly moved as a gold earring and a diamond-encrusted eye-patch swam into focus. They were attached to a large head that was bending over him.

"Welcome aboard *The Black Fang*, me hearties! I'm Bo'sun Bones."

Ace quickly glanced around. Beside him, Swoop and Rocket looked dazed but un-injured. A ball and chain were fastened around their legs and wrists and they were huddled by the mainmast of the pirate ship.

Ace stared back at the vampirate who had just spoken. He saw a short, plump bat with a barrel-like stomach that stuck out over his trousers. Bo'sun Bones was wearing a scruffy coat with voluminous sleeves and lots of pockets that jangled as he moved.

"I am the ship's magician, entertainer and all-round *bon viveur*." As he spoke, a pack of playing cards suddenly appeared in his podgy fingers. Ace watched in astonishment as the bo'sun shuffled, cascaded and fanned them. "Got anything worth gambling? No? How about a drink?" The cards vanished as quickly as they had appeared and Bo'sun Bones waved a collection of bottles under Ace's nose. "Grog, fire water, bilge water?"

Ace shook his head. The Bo'sun sighed.

The bottles disappeared and were replaced by strange juggling balls – five shrunken skulls.

"I think it's about time you met our first mate," Bones said as he continued juggling. "Allow me to introduce Mr Leech."

A shadow fell across the fruitbats. It was cast by an immensely tall and thin pirate. Dressed all in black, the mate glided silently across the deck, green eyes glowing in his skull-like, scarred face. Rocket shivered as he felt the vampirate's gaze burrowing into his flesh.

"Don't be put off by appearances. Mr Leech has a heart of gold. He loves his pets," the bo'sun said.

What sort of pets did the monstrous mate keep? Ace had a horrible feeling he was about to find out. Sure enough, Mr Leech came closer. As he did, he sniffed back a drop of yellow liquid that had appeared at the tip of his nose. Swoop caught a horrible whiff as the vampirate opened his mouth, revealing a pair of brown-green fangs.

"Here we are, my beauties," the mate said, opening a large tin. Wriggling inside it were ten thirsty leeches!

Bo'sun Bones roared with laughter when he saw the expression on the fruitbats' faces.

"If you ever need anything, don't be too shy to ask. Me and the boys are at your service."

Everywhere the fruitbats looked, hanging from the rigging, lining the ship's rail and kneeling on cannons, vampirates were staring menacingly back at them. They were all armed with sharp, pointed teeth. Rocket gulped. He hadn't realized quite what a bunch of bloodthirsty bite-throats they were up against.

"We're not scared of you," Ace said loudly.

"I agree," Rocket muttered below the loud guffaws of the pirates. "Terrified is more like it."

"You may have captured us," Ace continued, "but our friend escaped and will bring help very soon. You'll be in trouble when our army of attack bats arrives. But I'm a reasonable person and I'm willing to do a deal. If you let us go and leave quietly, we'll forget about this little incident. Now if you'll just unlock these chains—"

Ace stopped at the point of a cutlass that Bo'sun Bones had magicked into his hand like a conjuror's wand.

"Not so fast," Mr Leech hissed with breath that would have knocked an albatross out of the air at 1,000 metres. "I wouldn't count on your friend bringing help. Look!"

The fruitbats gasped as a soggy orange object was held up. Speared on a dagger were Radar's earwarmers. Aunt Bathilda had knitted them herself and given them to him with the warning, "You'll catch your death of cold without them. I don't expect thank-yous. I know you'll wear them, or else!"

In an effort to save his sky-cred, Radar had come up with a plan. He always kept the earwarmers in his pocket ready to pull on hastily if he flew into Bathilda. How had the vampirates got their claws on them? What had happened to Radar?

Bo'sun Bones seemed only too happy to tell them. "At first your friend's strange flying style took the pursuing pirates by surprise, but they soon caught up with him. They were closing fast when he fell out of the sky and crashed into a waterfall. They waited in case he surfaced, but there was no sign of him except these charming earwarmers. They were floating in the water."

"You cowardly creeps!" Swoop's shouts were drowned under a wave of piratical laughter. He struggled to wriggle out of his chains, but in vain… At last he gave up and glowered at the deck.

"And now, if you've learned how to behave properly," Bo'sun Bones continued, "Captain Blood would like a few words." A mouth organ piped up a funeral dirge as the fruitbats were lifted to their feet and paraded along the deck. They were pushed towards the stern of the boat and left at the bottom of a flight of wooden steps. They looked up nervously.

Close to, Captain Blood seemed even bigger than when the fruitbats had first seen him. A large admiral's hat was perched on his head and he was wearing a blue coat with heavy gold trimming on each shoulder. He was stroking something gently which he held in his left hand. Swoop shuddered when he made out what it was – a black, hairy spider.

"So, you are the fruitbats foolish enough to spy on Captain Blood and the Black Fang Gang, the greatest bataneers that ever sailed the Seven Seas! And you thought you would catch us napping while we only had a skeleton crew on watch?" The captain smiled. "Just my little joke, you understand. Now, what shall we do with you three?"

"Make 'em walk the plank! They look like shark bait to me."

"They look more like sardine bait to me. They're skinny specimens, all but one."

"How about some keel-hauling practice?"

"Now lads, what about your manners? We could always do with some fresh blood aboard ship. Why don't we ask our guests if they'd like to join us?"

"And become pirates?" Ace shouted loudly. "Over my dead body!"

Mr Leech licked his fangs and stared at the fruitbats. "Oh, good. I hoped you might say that," he hissed.

Rocket rubbed his neck worriedly as Captain Blood roared with laughter.

"I'm afraid you will have to curb your appetite for a while, Mr Leech. I think it would be a shame for them to miss our greatest triumph. You are probably wondering what we are doing here and I will tell you. I have been observing the preparations for your Fruit Festival with great interest. In a few hours, your Flight Leaders will bring out a vast treasure of rubies, gold and pearls. That treasure belongs to me, and I shall get it back."

Swoop looked puzzled.

"But how can it be yours? It was washed up on our island a hundred years ago."

"You dare question me?" Captain Blood shouted. He leapt furiously to his feet and a frightened gasp rose from the crew. Swoop hardly dared watch the huge bat struggle to control his anger. After what seemed like hours, the vampirate slowly sat down. "You think it couldn't be mine because I don't look a day over thirty years old," he smiled menacingly. "Well, I haven't looked any older than this for two hundred years."

Captain Blood ignored the fruitbats' gulps and continued.

"I plundered the treasure chest with its ten keys from a galleon. I had never seen such riches – worth a king's ransom – and always kept them in my coffin. Until one black night we sailed into a terrible storm. I abandoned my ship and treasure just before they sank. Since then I have been sailing the oceans, terrorizing and looting. Oh, I've enjoyed myself, really painted the seas red, but at the back of my mind I always wondered what had happened to my treasure-chest. Would it ever surface again? As soon as I heard about your festival, I knew where it had fetched up. That treasure shall be mine again!"

The vampirate brought his fist down on the ship's rail.

"As soon as the Flight Leaders are out of their caves, I shall strike. Our attack will be a total surprise. My cannons are loaded with grapeshot. A few rounds will stun your fellow bats, leaving us free to take them prisoner and to remove our booty. All that hard work will make me and the lads hungry, so we shall have our own party. Not so much a Fruit Festival – more a Fruitbat Festival. And it's so good of your friends to supply the garnish – blood oranges!"

Swoop looked in horror at Ace and Rocket. So that was the vampirates' fiendish plan! They had to be stopped, and the bats on Fruit Isle had to be warned, but how?

While thoughts raced through the fruitbats' minds, Captain Blood barked out orders.

"Search them and take them to the brig. I don't want any more disturbances. If anyone makes any mistakes, I'll tie them to the mast and make 'em take the dawn watch."

The crew suddenly went quiet and to a bat they turned white at this threat. Mr Leech broke the silence.

"Let's get on with the search," he hissed, cracking his knuckles.

While Bo'sun Bones' light fingers deftly searched the two others, Swoop squirmed under the mate's clammy touch. His hands felt like hairy centipedes running over his skin.

A few seconds later, the contents of the fruitbats' pockets were in a pile on the deck.

"It's all worthless rubbish," Bo'sun Bones said, but Ace spotted his watch and pocket money heading into the pirate's pockets.

"Hey, those are mine!" Rocket cried as the mate picked up the four ID cards Rocket had drawn. He broke off as Mr Leech stepped towards him.

"Our bo'sun isn't the only one who can do card tricks," he scowled. "Here are four cards, now there's eight, and now sixteen." The vampirate ripped the cards and held them over the ship's side. "And now they've disappeared. Ha, ha!"

The trio could only watch as the rest of their belongings followed the scraps of paper. Swoop's favourite sunglasses, Ace's champion conker and Rocket's secret snacks were all kicked overboard.

As they splashed into the water, heavy hands gripped the fruitbats' shoulders. They were pushed through a creaky door and taken below deck by the gruesome twosome, Bones and Leech. Their journey down into the depths of the ship was accompanied by a loud ticking noise.

"What's that?" Swoop asked. "Death watch beetle? This barnacled bucket's probably infested." The bo'sun chuckled.

"That's the captain's clock you can hear. He's very partial to it, is the captain. We always need to know the time."

Before Swoop could work out why, a loud BONG! rang through the ship. *The Black Fang*'s creaky timbers shivered and the fruit-bats were flung from one side of the narrow corridor to the other.

"You'll soon get used to the clock striking. It won't ruin your beauty sleep," sneered Leech. "Get going through the door on the left."

The trio found themselves in a long dark cabin. Through the gloom they made out shapes – strange boxes were tied on ropes between pillars. Loud snoring echoed from the boxes, making them sway slightly. The fruitbats followed the first mate as he threaded his way through the darkness. Ace glanced into one of the boxes – inside was a sleeping vampirate.

Ace realized what they were. "Hammock-coffins!" he whispered. Swoop and Rocket nodded slowly.

At the end of the cabin they were pushed down more steps. Rocket wrinkled his nose as they passed the galley, then Bones stopped suddenly and bent down. SCREECH! Rusty hinges protested as he hauled up a trap door.

"This is where you stay," he chuckled. "In you go."

Swoop stood on the edge, peering down into darkness. "But—" He never finished what he was going to say as he was given a hefty shove. Swoop fell through the air and landed with a dull thud. Seconds later, Ace and Rocket followed.

"Owww! Ouch!" protested Swoop. "Get

off, will you? I've heard of being the fall-guy, but this is beyond a joke."

Up above, the trap door slammed shut, showering the fruitbats with dust. Once the coughing and spluttering died down, Bo'sun Bones' eye-patch appeared through the bars in the door.

"I'm sure you'll settle in comfortably," he chuckled. "No one has ever complained before. We vampirates are famous for putting the word 'hospital' into our hospitality. In fact, to celebrate your capture, the Captain's ordered us to break out the grog – a nip each of crab-apple cider. It's got a real bite to it. Tomorrow evening we'll be launching a broadside on your friends. That'll give you something to ponder on. Ha! Ha!"

The Bo'sun's laughter echoed along the deck before slowly fading. The brig was pitch black – dark even for a bat. Bilge water sloshed below and Rocket heard something scratching on the planks. "What's that?" he squeaked.

"I hope it's not any of Leech's pets," Ace replied grimly.

"For a split second, I thought it might be someone coming to rescue us," Rocket said sadly. "Someone like Radar."

The fruitbats lapsed into silence.

"It's my fault," Swoop said. "If he'd stuck with me he'd still be alive. I know he wasn't a great flyer, but he meant well."

"This isn't the time to mope," Ace interrupted. "If anything we must escape for his sake, so his last flight won't have been in vain. He wouldn't have given up – he would have had some escape plan, however ridiculous."

"Well, what do you suggest then, oh great leader?" Rocket asked.

"How about using you as a battering ram?" Ace suggested. "Yeuch! Look down there."

The fruitbats stared down at a huge rat licking its lips hungrily.

"He-e-elp!" Rocket yelled, but there was no reply from the vampirates. The fruitbats heard the sounds of heavy footsteps, glass smashing and shouting from the decks above. Seconds later, a dreadful wailing sound echoed throughout the boat.

"This is agony," Rocket groaned, trying to block his ears. "Call off the torture. What are they doing? It sounds like they're murdering something."

Swoop nodded slowly.

"They *are* murdering something – a tune. They're singing. Listen, if you can stand it." At that moment the crew launched into a chorus with the strength of a Force Ten typhoon.

What shall we do when we capture the fruitbats?
Steal their booty and drink their blood.
Steal their booty and drink their blood.
Early in the morning.

"Talk about a secret weapon!" Rocket winced. "They've even frightened off the rats."

"But for how long?" Swoop muttered grimly. "We're in a fix. We must get out of here and warn everyone on Fruit Isle."

"Then we can eat," Rocket interrupted. "I'm starving. It makes my heart bleed thinking of all that lovely food back home."

"Just be thankful it's not your neck," Ace replied grimly. "And while you've been talking, I've been planning our escape. We've got two options. Both are risky and fraught with danger, but we must proceed with one of them. Option A is to try and open the trap door above, then sneak out through the ship while the pirates are still carousing. Option B is to break open that porthole and squeeze through it. The danger with this plan is that Rocket won't actually fit through the porthole."

"Very funny! Your tongue's almost as sharp as Blood's cutlass," Rocket grimaced. "Still, I hadn't noticed the porthole before – it's got some sort of shutter on the outside."

"I spotted that earlier," Swoop muttered thoughtfully. "There are similar covers everywhere – that's why the ship is so dark."

Ace cleared his throat noisily.

"This is all very interesting, but it hardly helps us get out of here. I suggest we vote on which escape option to try. I want a show of hands. All those who want option B... Oh, dear!" Ace's voting system stopped abruptly as the fruitbats tried to raise their arms. He had forgotten about the heavy chains around their wrists – they couldn't fly with them on. He paused for a second before continuing undaunted. "Just a temporary glitch. We'll soon get out of these. They don't call me Ace the great escapologist for nothing! Watch."

Swoop didn't like to mention that they wouldn't call Ace the great escapologist even if he paid them. Instead, he and Rocket watched as Ace's colour changed from brown to red and then to purple. The chains remained in place. At last he gave up.

"Well, at least I tried," he panted. "Has anyone else got any ideas?"

Nobody had. The fruitbats were silent. By now the top decks of the ship were quiet too as the vampirates slept off their grog, leaving the fruitbats alone with their thoughts.

In the darkness of the brig they were plunged into gloom. They had failed. They would never warn the others on Fruit Isle and the vampirates' attack would be a total success. Captain Blood would win another victory and live up to his name. At last, exhausted after their encounter with the vampirates and rocked by the gentle motion of the boat, the fruitbats felt their eyes growing heavy…

Swoop didn't know how long he had been asleep when suddenly his ears pricked up. Within a second he was bolt upright.

"What's that?" he hissed. He nudged the others. "Wake up. I heard something – there it is again! Listen."

"Get off me! It's probably Rocket's stomach or the rats."

"No … I think it's coming from outside. Look at the porthole – it's opening!"

The fruitbats stared as the porthole slowly opened. The shutter outside had already been removed and pale light streamed in round a dark shape as it clambered into the brig. Ace, Rocket and Swoop gasped.

Squeezing through the porthole, teeth clenched in a grimace … was Radar!

Chapter 7

Groaning horribly, the apparition heaved itself out of the porthole and shot across the cabin like a cork out of a bottle.

"It's a ghost! Keep away!" Ace wailed. "What do you want? Leave us alone."

The spooky spectre floated back towards the fruitbats.

"Hold on a second. It's me, Radar! I'm alive, not a ghost."

"But how did you—? We were told that you crashed into a waterfall."

"I did. I'd just done a Swoop Special Spin

and sideways glide as well. I lost consciousness and woke up in a cave that was hidden behind the waterfall. I couldn't see out and I didn't want to risk flying straight into a trap, so I began to explore the cave. After a few minutes I heard this awful off-key singing. I followed my ears and guess where I ended up? Looking down on *The Black Fang*! This whole island is riddled with caves, passages and tunnels. I could see the vampirates singing and dancing on deck. I waited until they started falling over and falling asleep then I flew over to rescue you."

"How did you find us?"

"That was easy," Radar said, grinning. "I followed the sound of Rocket snoring. Now it's my turn to ask questions. Why are you being held prisoner, and what exactly are the vampirates doing here? What do they want?"

Swoop quickly explained the piratical plans of Captain Blood and his crew. Radar turned white. The vampirates had to be foiled.

"I agree," Ace hissed. "No one on Fruit Isle knows about the vampirates, so it's up to us to tell them. First we've got to get out of these chains. What tools have you brought?"

Oh, dear! Radar hadn't thought of that. He looked at his feet in embarrassment.

"Some rescue this is!" Ace groaned. "It's back to the drawing board. We've tried pulling at these chains but they're far too strong. What else can we do?"

Radar picked a stone off the deck. He was about to use it as a hammer when Ace stopped him with a warning hiss.

"If you use that the guards will hear. Any other bright ideas?"

"I could pick the locks," Rocket suggested. "But only if my hands were free and I had a hairpin or a sharp piece of metal."

"Of course!" Swoop yelled excitedly. "Radar, check in my secret pocket. Leech missed it when he searched me. Inside is the Fruit Gang badge I made – it's got a metal pin. Try that, but be careful. Don't cut yourself or the vampirates will smell blood and come flying."

Radar's hand shook as he inserted the pin into the padlock fastening Rocket's chains. There was a dull click and the chains rattled to the floor. Rocket took over from Radar and a few expert turns of the pin later, the fruitbats were stretching their aching wings.

"How come you're so good at doing that?" Ace asked.

"It's easy," came the guilty reply. "We've got the same locks on the cake tin at home."

"That's something Bathilda doesn't need, eh, Radar?"

"Don't remind me," Rocket groaned loudly. "I thought I was never going to fly again."

"You still might not unless we're all quiet," Ace whispered. He beckoned to the gang to huddle around him. "OK, Step One of my escape plan has succeeded – we're out of those chains. Now for Step Two. Our captors are woozy at the moment, so we must take advantage of that and get off the ship before they recover."

DONG! DONG! *The Black Fang* shivered to its creaky timbers. Radar hit the roof with fright. He was only talked down after Ace explained about Captain Blood's clock.

"Time's running out," Ace continued. "Soon the vampirates will be weighing anchor and taking up battle stations. Let's move out through the porthole."

Swoop's arm shot out to stop Ace.

"I've got an idea. If we can get to the clock and turn it back an hour we'll buy more time to fly back and warn everyone on Fruit Isle. Who's game?"

"Confuse the enemy with the old time-switch tactic?" Ace nodded wisely. "It's a good plan. I'm surprised *I* didn't think of it. Let's go!"

Rocket reached through the bars on the trap door. The lock posed no problem for him and his pin.

As soon as the fruitbats fluttered out of the brig they could hear the sound of ticking coming from the decks above. The noise mingled with creaking planks and sploshing of water in the hold. It was almost as though the ship was a live thing – a wild animal that was waiting to wake up and pounce on the Fruit Gang.

Radar kept glancing nervously over his wing as they glided stealthily through the ship, up a flight of steps and past the sleeping quarters. Snores and sea-shanties rose from the hammock-coffins, rocking the ship and making the sleepers sway.

"Hand over your treasure! The game's up, you scurvy swabs!"

The fruitbats froze as a familiar figure appeared, blocking their way. Advancing unsteadily, his eye-patch skew-whiff, clutching a bottle in one hand and wielding a cutlass in the other – it was Bo'sun Bones.

"So you won't surrender? Take that!" The

pirate swung his cutlass back, and it hit the low roof beam above and stuck in the wood. "Curse you!" he roared. "There's not enough room to swing a cat o' nine tails here. Stand and fight like bats!"

"W … we surrender," Radar quavered.

"If you let us have some of that grog," Rocket suggested eagerly.

The Bo'sun suddenly collapsed and lay chuckling on the floor. Swoop realized what was going on.

"Look at his eyes – he's sleepfighting. Come on. Leave him alone. Let's get to the clock."

The gang stepped over the slumbering pirate and, following their ears, reached their destination. Standing in an enormous empty cabin, they looked up in awe at the gigantic clock that towered above them.

The main part of the clock was shaped like a coffin, supported on skull-shaped feet. A snarling pirate pendulum swung from left to right in front of two weights shaped like treasure chests. Rocket shivered at the picture on the clock face – *The Black Fang* in battle. Two daggers took the place of hands, pointing out the time.

Swoop took off and hovered in front of the clock face. He pulled at the minutes dagger … nothing happened. He strained again, but still couldn't shift it. It was too heavy for him to move while he was flying. If Swoop couldn't do it, what hope was there for the others?

"There *is* a solution." As usual Ace had a plan. "Time for the bat ladder routine. I will anchor myself to the ledge above the clock face. Radar will hang from my shoulders, Rocket from his, and Swoop will hold on to Rocket. That way, with his feet secure, he can get a better grip on the clock hands."

No other alternative sprang to mind. The bats prepared to take up positions. Ace soon recovered from Radar's first attempted landing, and when Swoop dropped perfectly on to Rocket's shoulders the ladder was complete. All the bats took the strain – they wobbled for a second but stayed firm.

Swoop pushed with all his strength at the dagger. At last a dull grinding noise signalled success. The fruitbats fluttered down and stared at their handiwork – the clock had gone back an hour.

"That should do the trick," Ace smiled. "Let's get out of here."

The fruit gang peered out of a cannonport. Their problems weren't over yet. Even if they got off the boat unnoticed they still had to get out of the cave. It wasn't going to be easy. The vampirates were bound to have guards posted at the main way out and at the exit the fruit-bats had discovered. Radar broke the silence.

"They won't have the waterfall covered. Follow me – I know the way."

Chapter 8

"I had a hunch that relying on Radar's sense of direction would lead to trouble. Let's face it, we're totally lost."

Ace was right, but that wasn't all. The fruitbats were also cold and tired and one of them was very hungry. As well as losing the way they had also lost all track of time. At first everything had gone to plan. They had slipped away unseen from *The Black Fang* and squeezed after Radar into a small tunnel. They had flown swiftly between the rocks until suddenly they hit trouble. The tunnel divided into three. Radar ransacked his memory, but he couldn't remember which one led to the waterfall.

The bats began exploring each tunnel in turn, only to find that while one soon ended in a solid wall of rock, the other two split up and led to caves with more passages leading from them. After what seemed like hours of fruitless flying, the bats clustered together. Time was running out, the vampirates might already be sailing into the attack and the Fruit Gang were powerless to prevent it.

"Ssssh! What's that?" Radar glanced round fearfully. He thought he had heard something, a strange rumbling from the depths of the rocky earth. Was it some sort of monster they had disturbed in its subterranean lair? No, it was Rocket's stomach rumbling.

"What can we do?" Ace asked. "We've tried following our instincts and it's got us nowhere. If we don't get out of here soon I don't think we'll ever see nightlight again."

"We'll starve to death and our ghosts will haunt Black Isle for ever."

"Don't worry, Radar…" began Swoop. "Hold on a second – look at Rocket. What's happened to him?"

Something had certainly had a strange effect on the large fruitbat. Rocket was standing bolt upright. Veins stood out on his face, his eyes were glazed over and his nose twitched.

"Follow me!" he growled. Slipstream whistled as he took off and flew so quickly that even Swoop had trouble keeping up.

"He must have got cave fever," Swoop thought until he felt a warm breeze blowing towards him. Seconds later, dim light appeared at the end of the tunnel. Rocket had done it! He had found a way out. How?

The fruitbats discovered the answer when they emerged blinking into the moonlight and found Rocket happily tucking into the fruits of a bramble bush beside the exit.

"Instead of following my instinct," he grinned broadly, "I decided to follow my nose. I can smell food from miles away."

The fruitbats grabbed as much food as they could while avoiding the thorns. Still munching, they took to the air. They had to eat on the wing as there was no time to lose. Ace and Swoop swept low over the calm sea that lay between them and Fruit Isle. Would they be in time to warn everyone?

Everything seemed normal as they sped through the sky. Up ahead the island was quiet, and there was no sign of any vampirates. Everything was calm and peaceful.

"I think our plan was successful," Ace gasped. "Give them a warning whistle, Rocket. That will soon wake them up."

Rocket let rip with one of his ear-splitting specials. The fruitbats flew over the mountain and dived down to their caves. Swoop pulled up suddenly. No sign of life emerged from their dark homes, no welcoming bats rose up to meet them. The only sound that reached their ears was the fading echo of Rocket's whistle. Ace and Rocket peeled off to check their caves. They were empty, as were all the others.

Meanwhile, Swoop had flown down to the beach where the festival was held. It was totally deserted. Not only was there no crowd of hungry fruitbats, but there was no sign of the banners, the bunting or the folding tables that should have been set up by this time. Even the old cargo ship, *The Golden Apple*, that was normally pulled up on the beach, was gone.

Radar's heart sank. They were too late and it was his fault. What should he do now? He wanted to crawl into a hole and disappear for ever. Why couldn't he be more like Ace or Swoop, or even Rocket? They would never have got lost under Black Island.

While he had led the others round and round in circles, the vampirates had attacked the fruit festival. It had obviously been a total success – they had taken the treasure and the fruitbats away. Even Aunt Bathilda must have been captured. For a second, pity for the vampirates flitted through Radar's mind, but it was quickly shoved aside as Ace gathered the gang together.

"We mustn't give up hope yet," he began. "Something's wrong. I know there's no sign of the fruit festival but there are no signs of a struggle either. If Captain Blood and his creepy crew had attacked, surely there would be some evidence – some damage? But there's nothing."

"Oh, yes, there is!" Swoop emerged from Radar's cave, waving a tatty piece of paper. "It's good news. This is a note to Radar from Bathilda. After the usual, um, questions as to where we are, she's written: 'So many bats arrived tonight that it was decided to move to a less crowded location. My suggestion of the beach at Half Moon Bay was warmly greeted by all. I personally supervised the loading of our boat, *The Golden Apple*, with fruit, but despite my excellent directions we have set off rather late. I shall expect to see you on the beach, wearing your earwarmers, and with a good reason for your disappearance.' "

Radar gulped while the others cheered. Maybe it would be all right after all. By switching the location of the festival, the fruitbats might escape the vampirates and scupper Captain Blood's plans.

"But we must still warn everyone that the vampirates are around," Ace said. "Come on!"

The Fruit Gang switched to vertical take-off mode. They blasted up high into the sky and scanned the horizon. Ace spoke first. "I can see Half Moon Bay. And there's our boat."

"But look to your left," Swoop added seriously. "That large dot is the vampirates. They've just sailed out of Black Island."

"Well, let's go then! What are you waiting for?" Ace shouted.

Rocket hovered hesitantly.

"I don't want to sound stupid or scared or anything, but how are we going to rescue everyone? If we just fly over there unarmed, we'll be caught again along with everyone else. The vampirates have got cannons and cutlasses. What have we got?"

The fruitbats stopped in their tracks. Rocket was right – how could they attack the vampirates and rescue their friends? The Fruit Gang didn't have a single weapon between them. What could they take? Ace began to regret swapping his water pistol for the book *The A – Z of Leading a Gang*, while Rocket wished that he had fixed his catapult as he had been meaning to. Swoop felt the sickening taste of defeat rise in his throat. Surely there must be something? Normally they could have thrown fruit at the vampirates, but there was none left on the island

– it had all been picked and loaded on to the fruitbats' boat.

"We could take the fruit that was dropped," Swoop suggested desperately. "There are a few bananas and peaches on the beach."

Fruit, fruit, fruit. The word bounced and ricocheted inside Radar's mind. Suddenly he had a brainwave. He knew exactly what they could take. They *did* have a secret weapon. He was about to speak out when he bit his tongue. What would the others think of his idea? Maybe it was a stupid suggestion, like most of his seemed to be. What should he do? Radar hopped from one foot to the other as he tried to make up his mind. At last he plucked up courage. If he didn't say anything now it would be too late.

"I've got an idea," he piped up nervously. "We can use Aunt Bathilda's fruit cakes!"

Chapter 9

In the stunned silence that followed his suggestion, Radar heard his heart pounding furiously. "What did you say?" Ace asked.

"Oh, it was nothing," Radar mumbled nervously. "Just an idea."

"Just an idea, just an idea – it's brilliant! It's exactly what we want. Where are the cakes?"

"It is? Oh, yes, of course it is." Radar tried to cover up his surprise before leading the trio into his cave. They rooted through the darkest, dustiest and dampest nooks and crannies to find the cakes.

"Well done," grinned Rocket as they safely stowed the secret weapons in bomb bags. "These will make a big difference."

Rocket was right but not in the way that he meant. It was a different Radar who, almost gracefully, took off with the others.

"I had a good idea," he thought. He was glowing with happiness and he somehow felt lighter, as if a weight had been lifted off his shoulders. The extra flying had made him stronger too – now he could easily keep up with the others. In his eagerness to see how his fruitcake idea would work, Radar almost overtook a surprised Ace. The Fruit Gang headed straight for the two converging dots on the horizon.

Before they had flown halfway towards the boats, the fruitbats were hit by an awful crashing and wailing.

"Yeowww!" winced Swoop. "What's that?" It was like flying into a barrier, like head-butting a solid wall of sound. The fruitbats were buffeted and pushed backwards. What was going on? What evil weapon were the vampirates using now? Ace's brainwaves were scrambled momentarily, but at last he worked out the cause of the terrible noise – it was music. Some of the vampirates must have formed a band. They had mistuned up and were playing the fruitbats into surrender.

"Now I know what they mean by a howling gale," Ace shouted. "At least they haven't started singing!"

"I never thought I'd miss Bathilda's earwarmers," Radar thought, "but right now they would be handy, or ear-y." His grin quickly disappeared as he gritted his teeth to plough into the sound storm.

Swoop peered at the horizon ahead. He made out the two different boats and he saw the nautical manoeuvring of each. The fruitbats had spotted *The Black Fang* and were trying to turn. The treasure was too heavy to airlift to safety so the fruitbats had to stay with the ship and try and outrun the vampirates.

But *The Golden Apple*, weighed down by her cargo, was slow to respond to the helmsbat. *The Black Fang* quickly closed down on its prey, the figurehead's arms grasping for its latest victims. The Fruit Gang were still only distant onlookers as the vampirates drew alongside the fruitbats' boat. BOOM! BOOM! BOOM! BOOM! BOOM! The pirates launched a five-cannon broadside of grapeshot.

The Golden Apple staggered and lurched to port. The crew were thrown sideways, clinging grimly on to anything solid. Slowly, very slowly, the ship righted itself, but its sails were in tatters, its rigging ragged, and its decks splattered with soggy goo. Scarcely before the bats aboard could recover their feet, they were sent reeling by another assault – grappling irons hooked the ship and a horde of snarling vampirates flew to the attack.

By now the Fruit Gang had nearly reached the ships. They could recognize familiar faces on both sides. Ahead and below, the fruitbats were being pushed back across the deck. Amongst the confusion, Radar spotted a familiar figure. Aunt Bathilda was holding firm against all-comers.

"Take that, you villain!" she said. She was swinging a strange but formidable weapon. Radar just caught sight of the words "Fruit Isle Wel—" before his banner was brought crashing down on the head of a vampirate.

"I bet that's one welcome he wasn't expecting," Radar grinned.

"Look there!" Radar followed Swoop's finger. The rest of the fruitbats were in trouble. Radar's brother was rapidly retreating as he fended off Mr Leech's cutlass thrusts with a table leg. Meanwhile, Bo'sun Bones was hurling daggers like a circus knife-thrower. Fruitbats were pinned by their clothes to the deck and the mast as Bones produced knife after knife from his sleeves. The Fruit Gang had to do something. Now they were on top of the action, Swoop was just about to dive down when Ace stopped him.

"We're armed but not ready. There's something extra we need – a plan of attack. Luckily this is my department and I have come up with a foolproof idea. A frontal attack is far too obvious so I've decided on a variation on the old pincer movement."

Ace saw the confused look on the others' faces as he explained, rattling out instructions like a machine gun.

"We'll split into two attack squads. Squad A will consist of Rocket and me, and Swoop and Radar will form Squad B. Squad A will start their fruit-bombing run and fly from the bows to the stern. Then Squad B will attack in the opposite direction. The entire future of Fruit Isle is on our shoulders. Good luck, everyone! Let's move out."

Swoop and Radar peeled off to the left, took up their positions and waited for Squad A to make their move. Ace and Rocket removed the fruitcakes from their bags before diving steeply down towards their target.

The vampirates were so busy below that none of them noticed the fruitbats till it was too late. Charred cherry-pie, rock-hard rock cakes and sultana surprises rained out of the sky on them. Radar saw a not so baked-well tart head for the pirate band who were playing on the poop deck. The tart went straight down the horn of a tuba, blowing the pirate player clean off the deck. More of Ace's fruit bombs scattered the band members who dived for cover, leaving their battered instruments behind. With a cry of "Chew on those!" Rocket's bombs landed on a cannon crew, splattering grapeshot ammunition among the vampirates.

Now it was Squad B's chance. It was time to attack while the vampirates were still dazed.

"Dive, dive, dive!" Wind whistled past Radar's ears as he followed Swoop. Down and down they flew. Swishing cutlasses glinted in the moonlight, as they darted in closer.

"I'll take Bo'sun Bones," hissed Swoop. "I've got a score to settle with him." Radar watched as Swoop gripped something tightly in his hand, feeling its weight. "Just right," he pronounced, letting go. He skimmed the scone, which bounced off three vampirates' heads and raced towards Bones. At the last minute the bo'sun saw the missile heading towards him. He tried to duck. Too late – the scone hit him amidships and he toppled over backwards into a cargo hatch. "Ha, ha!" Swoop yelled triumphantly. "Got him!"

Radar steamed in from the moon, but by now the vampirates were ready. A cannon roared, Radar darted left and the grapeshot flew harmlessly past. He controlled his wobbling wings and dived over *The Black Fang*.

"Wait, wait, wait," he muttered to himself. He knew who he was looking for. There, Mate Leech had his brother at his mercy. The vampirate stuck his cutlass into the deck and produced a tin. He was just about to set his pets loose on the fruitbat. Now! Radar let go his indigestible load.

"Dodge those if you can!" he yelled as his jammy dodgers fell from the sky, bang on target. Leech's eyes rolled up to the sky before he collapsed to the deck. Radar's brother blinked in shock. Suddenly he realized where he was. He spotted Radar and gave him the thumbs-up.

The fruitbats rallied as they saw the confusion amongst the vampirates. Ace, Swoop, Radar and Rocket joined in with their friends and began pushing their attackers back towards *The Black Fang*. Captain Blood roared furiously as he recognized his ex-prisoners.

"You meddlesome brats again! You'll wish

you were back in the brig by the time I've finished with you."

Ace smiled innocently, enraging the captain.

"Re-group, you swabs!" He blasted orders to his crew. "Come on, what's wrong with you? Don't let these land-lubbers beat you. We'll be the laughing stock of the seven seas."

But Aunt Bathilda was leading the fruit-bats' charge. Frightened vampirates leapt out of her way and flew back to *The Black Fang* for safety.

"Batten down the hatches!" yelled Bo'sun Bones before retreating into the towering stern decks. Swoop rapidly darted up to the top deck where he hovered just out of Captain Blood's range.

"I've got you in my sights!" yelled the fruitbat. He aimed a triple-layered pineapple upside-down cake. "This'll turn your plans upside down," Swoop grinned, hurling it with all his might.

But fast as lightning, the captain whipped

out his cutlass. SWISH, SWISH, SWISH! It flashed through the air, carving up the cake which landed neatly chopped on the deck.

"One slice or two?" the vampirate enquired, smiling, before his face suddenly clouded over with anger. "How would you like a taste of your own medicine?"

"Yikes!" Swoop gulped, ducking out of the way. The captain speared chunks of cake and tossed them back at the fruitbats. Now it was the vampirates' turn to cheer as they regained the upper hand. Spurred on by their captain's success, the crew emerged grinning from their hiding places. Captain Blood stretched out his wings and rose up into the sky, heading for *The Golden Apple*.

"Get those fruitbats!" he roared. "I want them, dead or alive!"

BOOM! BANG! The very air shivered as the vampirates' cannons spat out angrily. Wooden planks, dazed fruitbats and bits of masts flew across the decks. *The Golden Apple* staggered under the broadside and seemed to settle lower in the water. Radar felt a hand grasp his collar and heave him sideways – just in time. Grapeshot splattered against the bowsprit on which he had been leaning. "Thanks," he gasped.

"That's OK," Swoop replied. "We're not out of trouble yet." Vampirates were swarming on to *The Golden Apple*. Two dark shapes peeled off from the main attack and headed for Radar and Swoop. "Follow me!" Swoop yelled. Radar stayed on his tail as they took off, darting through masts and jinking around rigging in an effort to shake off their pursuers.

While Swoop and Radar were doing their mid-air manoeuvres, Ace and Rocket were helping out aboard the fruitbats' ship. A squad of pirates with swords and daggers bristling like a porcupine's spikes swept towards the duo. Ace delved deep into his bag and grabbed … nothing.

"Do something!" he yelled. "I'm out of ammunition."

"No problem, pardner," Rocket drawled in his best American accent. He stuffed his mouth full of banana-skin cake and chewed slowly. Closer, closer the vampirates came. Rocket braced himself. He waited until he could see the white of their fangs before unleashing a hail of guided-missile crumbs.

He was bang on target.

"Woah! Look out! Help!" The vampirates skidded out of control and swerved overboard.

But there was no time to gloat on Rocket's victory. All over the ship, similar skirmishes were taking place and the fruitbats were beginning to get the worst of them. Their makeshift weapons of table legs and planks of wood were no match for cold steel. Dodging a swinging boom and parrying a cutlass thrust, Ace raced over to reinforce the stern.

"Surrender! Resistance is futile!" They

were in mid-flight when the words appeared in Ace's brain. "Lay down your weapons." He struggled against the order, but his arms were obeying. It was Captain Blood! His spell was too powerful to fight.

Ace found himself lowering his bomb bag to the floor. All around, fruitbats were doing the same – except one! As a hairy vampirate bent down to pick up the discarded weapons, a plank of wood banged down on his head and a piercing voice rang out.

"Oh, no, you don't! Your hocus-pocus won't work on me. Pick up those weapons, or you'll have me to deal with."

Aunt Bathilda shattered Blood's concentration. His eyes glowed bright red with fury once he realized his spell had been broken. But he was not the type to give up easily.

"I'll still beat you," he hissed. In one swift movement, he darted in under the noses of the still-groggy fruitbats and kicked their weapons into the sea. Blood's triumphant cackle was just fading when Swoop and Radar landed on deck to help out.

"About time too," Bathilda called out. "You've got some explaining to do once this is over, young man."

Radar wasn't sure what was more frightening – facing his aunt or the vampirates? Still, the way the battle was turning he didn't think there would be much left of him after the vampirates had finished. The fruitbats were losing. They formed a defensive circle but they were outnumbered, out-manoeuvred and running out of ammunition.

Radar dodged a dagger-thrust from a huge, scarred pirate. He reached into his bag and pulled out a pair of Bathilda's sunglasses! He had forgotten about them – they weren't much help now. His opponent grinned as he lifted his dagger. Radar gulped and closed his eyes…

DONG! DONG! DONG! DONG! DONG! DONG! *The Black Fang* quivered as the clock struck six. With the sound still echoing in his ears, Rocket watched Captain Blood signal to his crew. The vampirates took off from *The Golden Apple* and hovered overhead like an ominous black cloud. Ace pulled Radar back into the circle. The fruitbats stared across to *The Black Fang* and found themselves looking straight down the barrels of five cannons. The silence that had settled over both ships was broken when Captain Blood's deep voice rang out across the water.

"Further resistance is useless. Surrender now." A dribble of saliva trickled down his fangs before he added triumphantly, "There is no escape."

Chapter 10

The Fruit Gang stared at each other unhappily. Was Captain Blood right? Was this really it, after all their struggles? Swoop ran through various escape options in his head. One by one he ticked them all off. The vampirates had covered every angle. He stared defiantly back at the cannons of *The Black Fang*, but in his heart he knew the fruitbats had lost. They had no more secret weapons, no hidden ace to play. This time there was no escape.

"Now I have you at my mercy," the captain

chuckled. "How I enjoy victory – it tastes so delicious. You are even bigger fools than I thought. To imagine you could defeat someone like me – the very idea is ridiculous."

As the fruitbats listened to Captain Blood's gloating, Swoop's sharp eyes noticed something happening behind the vampirates' ship. The sky was beginning to change colour. The fruitbats had been so busy fending off Blood and his creepy crew that they hadn't noticed the moon had disappeared. The starry night sky had gone and the first faint, pink glow of sunrise was visible on the horizon.

"We should have stayed in the brig," Rocket muttered. "It was safer there."

Swoop spotted the open shutter swinging against the brig porthole. He remembered how dark it had been inside. In his head he heard the clock ticking, something Bones had said and one of Captain Blood's threats. Suddenly Swoop's heart started beating faster. He nudged Ace.

"We may have one last chance. Look at the sky," he whispered. "We must stall the vampirates a bit longer. Pass it on to Radar and Rocket."

It was nearly dawn, what help was that? Before Ace could get Swoop to explain, Captain Blood continued with his victory speech.

"Victory brings its own problems, of course. I wonder what to do with you scurvy swabs. Should we take my treasure first and then enjoy our fruitbat feast, or the other way round? … Yes, what do you want?"

Swoop stepped forwards. He hunched his shoulders and looked down at the deck as he spoke.

"Please don't hurt us, sir. Take our treasure but leave us unharmed. Surely we are too insignificant for such a great pirate as yourself?"

Captain Blood roared with laughter.

"Do you hear that, lads? He wants us to

spare them. I do so enjoy this. Give me one good reason why I should let you go. And don't try to appeal to my better nature – I don't have one."

While Swoop racked his brains desperately, the rest of the Fruit Gang realized why he was playing for time. They had to help him out. An idea flashed through Radar's mind. There was no time to worry if it was good or not. Hoping that his knees weren't knocking, he took a step forward so he was next to Swoop.

"If … if you spare us we will tell the world of our encounter with you, the terror of the high seas," Radar stuttered. "But if none of us are left, who will know of your great exploits?"

Captain Blood looked thoughtful.

"A good answer," he mused. "It would certainly upset me if the world did not know of my dastardly deeds. The brilliance of my victory would go unnoticed, like the Battle for Shark Cove where I let the lucky ones walk the plank. That was a superb tactical victory, wasn't it, Bo'sun?"

"Oh, er, yes, sir," agreed the bo'sun. "Dressing Mr Leech up in women's clothes and having her signal for help was a stroke of genius. The expression on those fools' faces when they realized…"

While Captain Blood continued discussing his bloodthirsty battles, Ace glanced at the horizon behind *The Black Fang*. Already the first glimmers of sunlight were beginning to burn off the mist that was rising up off the sea. Just a few more minutes. If only the vampirates would keep talking for a few short minutes.

"Ahem!" Leech's dry cough interrupted the captain. "There is a simple solution, sir. We could let one fruitbat go free after they have done a few simple jobs about the boat. In the meantime, the crew, myself and my pets are feeling thirsty…"

"Of course, Mr Leech. And I want to get my hands on the treas—"

He never finished as Rocket rushed forwards and cowered on the deck.

"Me, me! Please choose me! I'm very useful. Look, I'll scrub your decks or mend the sails and I'll even haul up the anchor."

The vampirates cheered and laughed as Rocket tried to demonstrate what he could do. He fell over as he tried to clean the decks, then got himself hopelessly entangled in the sails and wrapped up in the anchor chain.

"Enough of this," Blood ordered after a few minutes. "I am growing impatient. My trusty crew, let the party begin!"

Rocket had done a brilliant delaying job. Before the vampirates could obey their captain's orders, Ace stepped forwards.

"I'd hate to ruin your party, but why don't you look behind you?"

Captain Blood smiled thinly.

"What are you talking about? I expected

something better than that pathetic 'behind you' trick. I know there is nothing behind us that can help you."

"Well, if you're so sure, then it won't hurt to look," Ace replied.

"What nonsense is this?" the captain snarled. He drew his cutlass in anger, then gradually calmed down. "However, let it never be said Captain Blood is not a true gentlebat. It is a simple wish, and seeing as it is your last request, I will do as you ask."

The vampirate whirled round viciously. What he saw turned his pale face even whiter. He staggered backwards.

"What…? How can it be dawn? Sunrise isn't for another hour. My clock is never wrong."

"That's what you think," Ace grinned triumphantly. "We turned the time back an hour before we escaped from your clutches. It looks like we've also turned the tables on you."

The crew of *The Black Fang* suddenly looked uneasy. Just then a ray of sunlight crept over the horizon and lit up a pirate in the crow's nest. One moment the fruitbats were looking at a large cutlass-waving vampirate, the next he disappeared in a puff of smoke.

The situation suddenly dawned on the vampirates. Panic-stricken, they dropped their weapons and stampeded back to their ship.

"Abandon attack!" yelled Bo'sun Bones. "Get out of the sun!" The vampirates pushed and shoved in their efforts to get under cover.

"Stand fast, you mutinous—" Blood's orders were drowned out by the mob. "I can't believe it," he hissed. "I've been tricked."

The fruitbats cheered at the chaos in front of them. All over *The Black Fang*, the crew fought each other as they dived into hatches and squeezed through portholes. At last Ace signalled for silence.

"It's time to strike home our advantage.

Now the Fruit Gang will swing into action."

"But what about the sun?" a voice piped up. "It'll blind you."

"Never fear," Ace said confidently. "Thanks to our star member, we are equipped for any emergency. Radar, issue the special anti-glare gear."

Radar looked confused. What was Ace talking about? Special anti-glare equipment? Maybe he had taken a knock on the head, or the sun was beginning to get to him.

"Look lively there," Ace continued. "Hand me the bomb bag."

"But there's nothing in it except for—" Radar broke off. "Except for the sunglasses." Of course, that's what Ace meant. Radar grinned broadly. His idea hadn't been so bad after all.

Ace winked as he chose the pineapple glasses. Seconds later the Fruit Gang were kitted up and ready to go. Before they took off, a familiar voice reached their ears.

"Radar, you take care of those glasses," Aunt Bathilda ordered. "And take care of yourselves."

The fruitbats on *The Golden Apple* quickly filed below decks while the Fruit Gang took to the air. Through their anti-glare equipment they saw that Captain Blood was the only figure left on the deserted decks of *The Black Fang*. Furiously he drew his sword and slashed the ropes joining the ships together.

"You haven't seen the last of me!" he screamed. "I'll be back." Blood's warning hung in the air after he dived into his cabin.

The fruitbats stared at each other – and grinned. Their glasses looked hilarious. Still, they did the trick. At last the sun rose over the horizon. The Fruit Gang hovered in the air for a second, then chorused: "BAT ATTACK!"

With their first swoop, they tipped *The Black Fang*'s cannons into the sea. Then they swung round and lashed the ship's wheel to send the vampirates back where they had come from. The tall ship began drifting off into the distance.

Having achieved their mission, they returned to cheers from inside *The Golden Apple*. Even Radar's big brother clapped him on the back.

After a few minutes, a hush settled over the ship. The crowds parted for a large bat to make her stately progress towards the Fruit Gang – it was Aunt Bathilda. What was she going to say?

"So, here you are at last!" Aunt Bathilda's voice was even more stern then before. Her severe expression gave nothing away. "You seem very pleased with yourselves. Well, let me recall your recent behaviour. You disappear for hours without explanation then when you do arrive, Radar, it is without earwarmers and with a selection of my finest cakes, pies and puddings to use as weapons. And now, no doubt you expect that I will forgive you..." Swoop and Radar exchanged nervous glances while the others shuffled their feet unhappily.

"Well, of course I do," Aunt Bathilda continued. Then, as Radar opened his eyes wide with surprise, his aunt smiled. "You saved our skins out here. Thanks to you, tomorrow night we'll have the best fruit festival these islands have ever seen. Well done!"

The bats laughed and cheered. Swoop showed off with some mid-air somersaults while Ace flew over the ship and did a victory roll. As the fruitbats steered their battered vessel back to shore, Radar looked over his shoulder. He scoured the horizon for *The Black Fang*, but it had disappeared from sight. No trace remained of their enemies except Captain Blood's last words, echoing in Radar's memory.

"Don't worry about those villainous vampirates," Rocket grinned. "They won't dare show their ugly mugs round here again. We've seen the last of them."

But Radar shivered. Somehow he wasn't so sure....

by R.L. Stine

Reader beware, you're in for a scare!

These terrifying tales will send shivers up your spine . . .

Available now:

Look out for: